To the children of the C. H. A. Projects
J. S. G
· · · · · · · · ·
To Lucille and Sammy and Laine
L. C.

Text copyright © 1971 by Lucille Clifton
Illustrations copyright © 1991 by Jan Spivey Gilchrist
Design © 1991 by Russell Gordon
All rights reserved, including the right to reproduce this
book or portions thereof in any form.
Published by Henry Holt and Company, Inc.,
115 West 18th Street, New York, New York 10011.
Published simultaneously in Canada by Fitzhenry & Whiteside Ltd.,
195 Allstate Parkway, Markham, Ontario L3R 4T8.

Library of Congress Cataloging-in-Publication Data
Clifton, Lucille.
Everett Anderson's Christmas Coming/Lucille Clifton;
illustrated by Jan Spivey Gilchrist
Summary: Relates, in verse, the excitement and joy of a young boy
anticipating as well as celebrating Christmas in the city.
ISBN 0-8050-1549-3
[1. Christmas—Fiction. 2. Apartment houses—Fiction. 3. Single-
parent family—Fiction. 4. Afro-Americans—Fiction. 5. Stories in
rhyme.] I. Gilchrist, Jan Spivey, ill. II. Title.
PZ8.3.C573EV 1991
[E]—dc20 91-2041

Henry Holt books are available at special discounts
for bulk purchases for sales promotions, premiums,
fund-raising, or educational use. Special editions
or book excerpts can also be created to specification.

Printed in the United States of America
on acid-free paper.∞

1 2 3 4 5 6 7 8 9 10

Everett Anderson's Christmas Coming

Lucille Clifton

· · · · · · · · ·

Illustrated by Jan Spivey Gilchrist

Henry Holt and Company
New York

DECEMBER 20

5 more days

Allen County Public Library
Ft. Wayne, Indiana

Everett Anderson
loves the sound
of Merry Christmases
all around

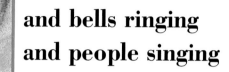

and bells ringing
and people singing

and Mama smiling her
secret smile
and winking at him
once in a while.

DECEMBER 21

Snow

In 14A
we live between
the snow that falls
on downer lives,
and from our window
we can watch
the early part
that mists and flies
and never the wet
and slushy one. Oh
14A is a blessing
says Everett Anderson.

DECEMBER 22

Window Shopping

If Daddy was here
I'd want a train
that could really go,
but he would know
if he was here.

If Daddy was here
I'd want a bike
with a real bell,
but he could tell
if he was here.

If Daddy was here
I'd worry him
the whole while,
but he'd just smile
if he was here.

DECEMBER 23

Everett Anderson
knows he should
be good
but it's the biggest ball,
he had to bounce it on the wall;
and when you climb on top the chair
you see the shelf and what's up there

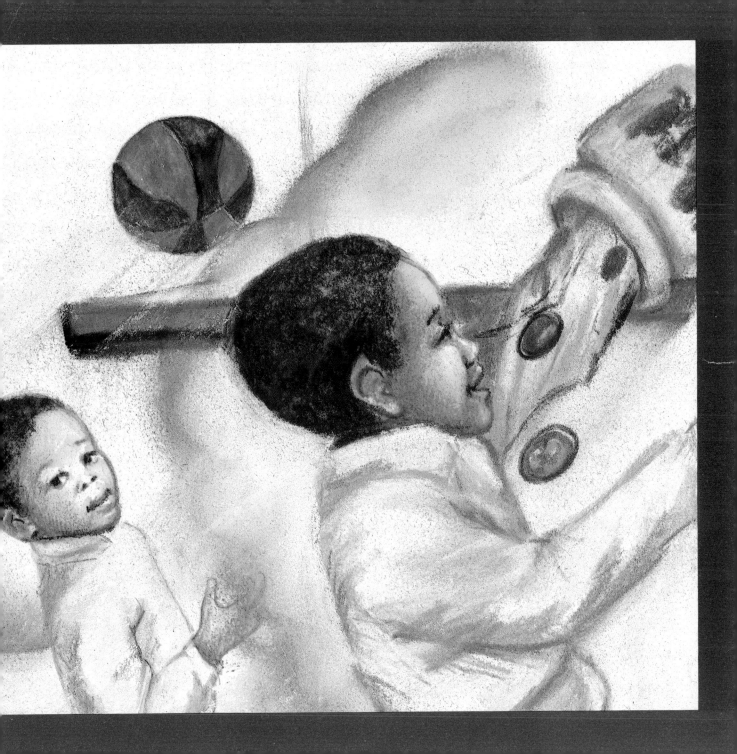

and everybody needs to know
why toilets flush and how
clocks go,
even when they're sure
they should
(like Everett Anderson)
be good.

The grown-ups come
and laugh
and clown
and talk real loud
and dance around
and drink their drink
and spill their ice
and Mama doesn't get mad.
In 13A they think it's bad,
but Everett Anderson thinks it's nice.

DECEMBER 24

A Tree in an Elevator

1 2 3 4 5 6 7 8 9 10 11 12 13 14 15

Whatever you think,
whatever you say,
a tree can grow
in 14A
and bloom with blue
and gold and pink
whatever you say,
whatever you think,
laughs the one who thought
it couldn't be done,
Everett Anderson.

DECEMBER 24

He understood about the inn.
He liked the barn and didn't care.
He thought it was the place to be
when He looked and saw His Mama was there,
thinks Everett Anderson.

DECEMBER 25

Christmas Morning

**Boys with lots
of boxes
smiles Everett Anderson
spend all day Christmas
opening
and never have much fun.**

DECEMBER 25

Christmas Night

14A
is up so high
our Christmas bounces
off the sky
and shines on all
the downer ones,
Merry Christmas to them
says Mama
Merry Christmas from me
says Everett Anderson.